Bad Dog

I Like to Read® books, created by award-winning picture book artists as well as talented newcomers, instill confidence and the joy of reading in new readers.

We want to hear every new reader say, "I like to read!"

_____

Visit our website for flash cards, activities, and more about the series:
www.holidayhouse.com/ILiketoRead
#ILTR
This book has been tested by an educational expert
and determined to be a guided reading level C.

Bad Dog

by David McPhail

I Like to Read®

HOLIDAY HOUSE • NEW YORK

In memory of Daisy: a good dog was she

I LIKE TO READ is a registered trademark of Holiday House, Inc.

Copyright © 2014 by David McPhail
All Rights Reserved
HOLIDAY HOUSE is registered in the U.S. Patent and Trademark Office.
Printed and Bound in February 2020 at Tien Wah Press, Johor Bahru, Johor, Malaysia.
The artwork was created with pen and ink and watercolors.
www.holidayhouse.com
10 12 14 16 18 20 19 17 15 13 11

Library of Congress Cataloging-in-Publication Data
McPhail, David, 1940-
Bad dog / by David McPhail. — First edition.
pages cm. — (I like to read)
Summary: "Sometimes, Tom is a bad dog. But he can be good, too!
His family loves him no matter what" — Provided by publisher.
ISBN 978-0-8234-2852-6 (hardcover)
[1. Dogs—Fiction. 2. Behavior—Fiction.] I. Title.
PZ7.M478818Bad 2014
[E]—dc23
2012038836

ISBN 978-0-8234-3298-1 (paperback)

Tom is my dog.
I love him.

But he can be bad.

He can make Mom mad.

He can make Dad mad.

He can make Kit mad.

Tom can be bad, bad, bad.

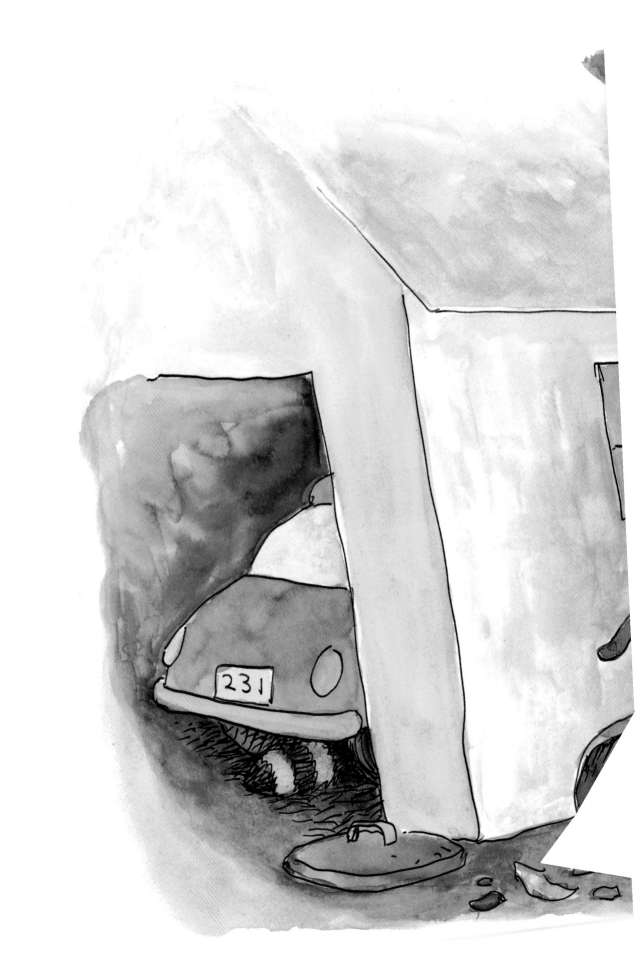

Dad says that Tom must go.

I am sad.

Oh, no.
Kit is gone.

Mom can't find Kit.

And Dad can't find Kit.

Tom wants me.

So I go.

I see Kit.

Mom and Dad come.
Tom is good, for now.

Tom is my dog.
I love him when he is good.
And I love him when he is bad.

You will like these too!

Boy, Bird, and Dog by David McPhail

Dinosaurs Don't, Dinosaurs Do by Steve Björkman

Fish Had a Wish by Michael Garland
KIRKUS REVIEWS BEST CHILDREN'S BOOKS LIST
AND TOP 25 CHILDREN'S BOOKS LIST

I Said, "Bed!" by Bruce Degen

Late Nate in a Race by Emily Arnold McCully

See Me Run by Paul Meisel
A THEODOR SEUSS GEISEL HONOR BOOK

Sick Day by David McPhail

See more I Like to Read® books.
Go to www.holidayhouse.com/I-Like-to-Read/

I Like to Read® Books in Paperback
You will like all of them!

Bad Dog by David McPhail

The Big Fib by Tim Hamilton

Boy, Bird, and Dog by David McPhail

Can You See Me? by Ted Lewin

Car Goes Far by Michael Garland

Come Back, Ben by Ann Hassett and John Hassett

The Cowboy by Hildegard Müller

Dinosaurs Don't, Dinosaurs Do by Steve Björkman

Ed and Kip by Kay Chorao

The End of the Rainbow by Liza Donnelly

Fireman Fred by Lynn Rowe Reed

Fish Had a Wish by Michael Garland

The Fly Flew In by David Catrow

Good Night, Knight by Betsy Lewin

Grace by Kate Parkinson

Happy Cat by Steve Henry

I Have a Garden by Bob Barner

I Said, "Bed!" by Bruce Degen

I Will Try by Marilyn Janovitz

Late Nate in a Race by Emily Arnold McCully

The Lion and the Mice by Rebecca Emberley and Ed Emberley

Little Ducks Go by Emily Arnold McCully

Look! by Ted Lewin

Look Out, Mouse! by Steve Björkman

Me Too! by Valeri Gorbachev

Mice on Ice by Rebecca Emberley and Ed Emberley

Pete Won't Eat by Emily Arnold McCully

Pig Has a Plan by Ethan Long

Ping Wants to Play by Adam Gudeon

Sam and the Big Kids by Emily Arnold McCully

See Me Dig by Paul Meisel

See Me Run by Paul Meisel
A THEODOR SEUSS GEISEL AWARD HONOR BOOK

Sick Day by David McPhail

3, 2, 1, Go! by Emily Arnold McCully

What Am I? Where Am I? by Ted Lewin

You Can Do It! by Betsy Lewin

Visit http://www.holidayhouse.com/I-Like-to-Read/ for more about I Like to Read®
books, including flash cards, reproducibles, and the complete list of titles.